The Return of
ARCHIBALD
GRIBBET

by Adèle Geras

Illustrated by Sumiko Davies

"The whole of tomorrow and tomorrow night and the whole of Sunday," said Nell, kicking the shingle so that the pebbles flew up in front of her and landed in the waves that were creeping up the beach. "It's just not fair. Shiny Sylvia and toffee-nosed Uncle Archibald ask us to stay and we have to go. I don't see why we should have to."

"Because Shiny's Mum's second cousin," said Mike, "and Aunt Hatty says that blood is thicker than water. That means you have to go and stay with horrible relations and be polite to them."

"But Shiny's such a distant relation," Nell sighed. "Not a proper one at all, really. I think Aunt Hatty ought to put her foot down, I bet if Mum and Dad were still alive, they'd never make us go there every month and eat those squishy, pale yellow, wobbly flans with bits in them, and be plonked in front of the video every five minutes, and be told to keep still while Shiny does her nails or lies under the sunlamp or puts smelly creams on her legs."

"I don't mind the video that much. I quite like it," said Mike. "And sometimes Uncle Archibald lets me look at his collection for a bit. You should come and have a look – it's a really ace collection."

"Stamps!" Nell snorted. "You and your stamps. You think he's being kind, but that's because you're too young to see what he's up to. He enjoys making you envious. He loves seeing your mouth drop open, hearing you go "Ooh" and "Aah". He knows you've got Dad's collection and he's trying to make out it's not as good as his. I hate him. His hands are like suet pudding."

"His eyes are like boiled gooseberries."

"His hair is all slick and black, like boot polish."

"What's his mouth like?" asked Mike.

"Like a goldfish's," said Nell. "Or a worm – pink and gaping at the same time. Ugh."

Mike began to laugh, and Nell laughed too for a moment, and then stopped.

"Come on, Mike," she said. "Let's go home. I promised Aunt Hatty we'd pack the case for tomorrow before tea."

"Oh, let's stay on a bit ... go on, please, Nell. It's nice now, all alone with the sea and nobody else here at all."

"OK," said Nell. "Just for a bit longer, then."

She stared out over the water, a silvery sheet in the hazy light of the October afternoon. The summer visitors in their "kiss-me-quick" hats and their slogan-printed T-shirts had all gone. The beach was deserted. Not a crisp bag nor an ice-lolly wrapper in sight, and the pier with pretty wrought-iron frills on all the roofs and railings, stood quietly in the water on its spindly wooden legs.

"I wish," said Nell suddenly, "I really wish that something would happen to make this visit different."

Mike wasn't listening.

"What's that, Nell?"

"Where?"

"Over there. It's shining in the sun. Can you see it? It looks green. There. Look."

"It's only a bottle."

"I'm going to get it."

"Whatever for? Someone must have left it behind after a picnic."

"There might be a message. It might have been thrown overboard thousands of miles away and drifted here all by itself."

"That's in stories!" Nell was scornful. "That's not true."

"I'm going to look anyway." Mike went down to the edge of the water, picked up the bottle, looked at it for a moment and waved it above his head.

"Nell," he shouted, "there *is* a message. Come and look ... quick. Come here and see."

Reluctantly, Nell rose to her feet and went to look at the bottle.

"It is a message, isn't it?" Mike was jumping up and down. "I told you, didn't I? From thousands of miles away."

"It's a message," Nell said, "but you don't know where it's from. It's probably just some tripper having a bit of a laugh."

"I'm going to take the cork out," said Mike. "Look, it comes out easily and I reckon ..." (Mike wriggled a finger into the mouth of the bottle) "... I reckon I can get the paper out. There!"

"Let me see," said Nell.

"Hey!" said Mike." Me first, I found it."

"Well, tell me what it says then."

"I can't understand it," said Mike. "It doesn't make sense. You look."

Nell looked. The note read:

I come where I am needed

"I don't understand it either," she said. "Who comes? Needed for what? It isn't even signed. That shows it's a trick if it doesn't make sense."

"I don't think it's a trick," Mike said quietly. "I think it's mysterious and spooky."

"Yeah, well, you would, wouldn't you?" Nell said. "It's dead simple and it makes no sense and we've got to go home and your shoes are sopping wet. Come on."

Mike put the note into his pocket, holding the green glass bottle carefully in both hands, he followed Nell up the beach. As he reached the steps to the promenade, he turned back to look at the sea, and he saw, he thought he saw, on the far horizon where the sea and the sky meet in a misty line, the silhouette of a clipper with all sails set.

"Nell," he began, puzzled, knowing that ships like that no longer sailed the seas.

"What is it?" asked Nell, already half way up the steps.

"Nothing," said Mike. The ship had vanished and Nell would never believe him. He must have imagined it.

Ever since the death of their parents in an aeroplane crash five years earlier, Nell and Mike had lived with their father's aunt, Hatty Fenton, in the Seaview Guest House (Bed and Breakfast, television lounge, children welcome, special rates for Senior Citizens). Between March and the end of September, Aunt Hatty's feet, as she was very fond of saying, never touched the ground, and five o'clock on summer afternoons was always particularly hectic. There were tables to be laid in the dining-room and the menu stuck on to the kitchen wall to be consulted, which colour soup tonight? Green or orange or brown?

From October to March, Aunt Hatty rested. She was resting now. Nell smiled at the sight of her curled up in the big armchair with a book called "The blood-stained bride of Castle Romayne".

Mike was sorting through his stamp album, admiring the squares and rectangles, the tiny pictures of bright birds, trains, kings and queens, flowers, bridges, animals, trees, all the bits and pieces of gummed paper. They lay in rows on the thick pages of the album like gems on a jeweller's tray.

The small suitcase had been packed and stood ready in the hall. This time tomorrow, Nell thought, we'll be sitting in that overheated lounge with Shiny Sylvia rattling her charm bracelets and Uncle Archibald pinging away on his calculator and the TV on full blast showing something that's considered suitable, like "Mary Poppins". The glass bottle stood on the table. "I wonder," thought Nell, "if it did come from thousands of miles away. It's a strange shape, and in the light it glows green and blue and turquoise like the sun shining through deep water. Lovely."

The door bell rang suddenly into the silence.

"Now who on earth can that be?" said Aunt Hatty crossly, looking up from her book.

"Shall I go and see?" asked Nell.

"Yes, all right dear," Aunt Hatty sighed. "Thank you."

Nell made her way through the dimly lit hall

and opened the front door. Standing on the steps was a tall, thin man wearing polished boots and a hat with a wide brim which threw a shadow over his face. He took his hat off when he saw Nell, and bowed like a prince in a pantomime. Nell curtsied back before she could stop herself, and felt like a fool.

She said, rather abruptly, "Good evening. Can I help you?"

"I believe you have lodgings ... rooms ... accommodation?"

"Yes," said Nell, "we do in summer, but the season is over now and well ... I think I'd better ask my aunt. She's in the back lounge. Would you follow me please?"

The man smiled, picked up an ancient black Gladstone bag, and stepped into the hall.

"My name," he said, "is Coronado."

Aunt Hatty's book lay on the carpet, quite ignored.
She was laughing and talking with the new guest
as if he were an old friend. They'd all had supper
on trays in front of the television and now the
sausages and mashed potatoes and baked beans
were finished, and Aunt Hatty was handing round
slices of Battenberg sponge and cups of tea.

"Nell," she said, "please pass this cup to Mr
Coronado."

Nell took the cup and was about to hand it to
their guest when Aunt Hatty cried, "Silly me! I
forgot to ask you if you take sugar, Mr Coronado."

"That's perfectly all right," Mr Coronado smiled
and waved his fingers in the direction of the
teatray. Instantly, two lumps of sugar floated out
of the sugar bowl, hovered for a few seconds
above the hearth rug and then plopped gently
into the cup Nell was holding. They did not even
make a splash.

"Hey!" said Mike as Nell, her hands trembling,
gave the cup to Mr Coronado as quickly as she
could.

"That's magic," Mike said. "That's like Paul Daniels. That's real proper magic. I saw it. Can you do more? How do you do it?"

Mr Coronado smiled. "There are a few ... things I can do. You pick up tricks like that when you travel as much as I do. From here and there and everywhere."

"Can you turn this into a flying carpet?" Mike patted the hearthrug that he was kneeling on. "Nell, come and sit here. Please, Mr Coronado, please make us fly."

"Well," said Mr Coronado, "if your aunt doesn't mind, I could perhaps try, although you know, I am a little out of practice."

Nell sat down besides Mike on the rug. Mr Coronado waved a hand above his head and the small carpet rose a few inches into the air.

"Can't it go any higher? Can't we fly out of the window?" Mike asked.

"Michael!" said Aunt Hatty sharply, "mind your manners and give over pestering Mr Coronado. I expect he's tired. And you and Nell together are a bit of a weight, I shouldn't wonder."

The hearthrug settled down again into its place near the fire.

"I told you," said Mr Coronado, "I am a little out of practice, and perhaps your aunt is right and you are a little heavy. No doubt we'll do better tomorrow."

"But we won't be here tomorrow," Nell and Mike said together. "We're going to visit our Mother's cousin, Sylvia."

"We won't be back till Sunday night," added Mike. "I wish we didn't have to go. They're both horrible."

"Get on with you," said Aunt Hatty. "That's no way to speak of your Mum's second cousin. Whatever will Mr Coronado think of you?"

"But they are horrible, Aunt Hatty. You know they are. All smooth and posh and … and well, horrible."

"Perhaps," said Mr Coronado, "I could come and see you there."

"But you haven't been invited," said Nell. "How will you get in? Would Shiny Sylvia let you come?"

"I have my methods," said Mr Coronado, "and if you would like me to come, then I would be delighted."

Nell clapped her hands. "Oh, that would be really terrific!"

"But you won't like it there, I warn you," said Mike. "The food's awful."

"Are you a magician?" asked Nell. "Have you ever been on TV?"

"Oh, no," said Mr Coronado, "not a real magician at all. A traveller, an explorer, a wanderer."

"We had a hypnotist here all summer once," said Aunt Hatty. "About two years ago it was ... he was appearing down at the Royalty Theatre. Well, the things he could make people do, you simply wouldn't believe!"

She laughed and then she and Mr Coronado began talking again as if flying sugar lumps and hovering hearthrugs were the most natural things in the world. Nell and Mike stared and stared at their amazing guest until bedtime, watching for more marvels, but none came and at last they went upstairs.

Most people live in houses. Archibald and
Sylvia Gribbet lived in a "desirable residence",
a large, square house set in an acre of tidy
lawns and rectangular flowerbeds where
rose bushes and hydrangeas grew quietly
and did as they were told.

Nell and Mike stood on
the doorstep.

"It's raining," said Mike. "It always seems to rain when we come here, almost on purpose so we can't go into the garden."

"There's not much to do in the garden anyway. Shiny Sylvia says we can play on the lawn, but she'll never let us kick a ball or stick stumps in for cricket in the summer. Even when we run, she frowns all the time."

"She'd probably like us to take our shoes off before we tread on it." Nell giggled. "It doesn't even look like real grass, most likely gets ironed instead of mown."

"Ring the bell," said Mike. "It's getting cold out here." Nell pressed a white button and the chimes of "When the Saints go Marching in" could be heard faintly from inside.

Shiny Sylvia opened the door.

"Darlings!" she cried as she gathered the children into her arms and pressed their faces into her pink, silky bosom, fragrant with expensive French perfume which reminded Nell of marzipan. "How gorgeous to see you!"

"Hello, Aunty Sylvia," said Nell, pulling away from the cutting edge of a diamond brooch.

"Come into the living room, dears, and sit down for a minute. I shan't offer you coffee because it'll be lunchtime ever so soon, and guess what?" She paused for effect.

"What?" Mike asked dutifully.

"Well, just for a treat, Uncle Archie will be with us for lunch today." She lowered her voice to a whisper and winked at the children. "He's got something very, very exciting and important to say to you. Now hang your coats up here ... oh, dear, poor Nell! Such a threadbare coat for my darling Vicki's little girl. Still, I suppose Hatty does her best, and when all's said and done, she's only a landlady, after all, and she is rather elderly, isn't she, so we shouldn't judge her too harshly."

"She's very healthy," said Mike. "I bet she lives for ages and ages."

"I daresay she will, dear," said Shiny Sylvia. "Now come on into the warm."

Nell and Mike sat anxiously down on the velvety orange cushions of the sofa. Everything in the Gribbets' house was either fringed, gilded, shiny or velvety. There were mirrors everywhere in gold frames. Chandeliers that tinkled, cigarette boxes that played tunes when you opened them, and lamps with beige shades and marble bases. The carpet was thick, fluffy and white, like warm snow, and Nell always felt it would get dirty if she so much as tiptoed onto it, but Uncle Archibald was fond of pouring ash and dirt all over it and

demonstrating with a vacuum cleaner how
miraculously it shed all possible filth, and how
everything the television commercial claimed for
this carpet was true.

Shiny Sylvia was yellow and highly polished to match her residence. She wore red, oily-looking lipsticks, and yellow bracelets that made a noise as she moved her arms. Her hair was yellow too, done up in a banana shape at the back and with a bunch of curls falling over her forehead. Her shoes were black and glittery and her tights rasped together as she walked. She wasn't exactly fat. It was more as if she'd got into skin that was a couple of sizes too tight for her and was bulging a little over.

Just in case there were not enough ornaments all over the house, Shiny Sylvia collected antique china and kept it in a glass-fronted cabinet in the living room. When Nell was very young she used to love standing in front of the glass, and looking at the delicate flowers and the pretty painted birds on the gold-rimmed plates, the little figures of shepherds in pale green coats and shepherdesses in gold slippers and pink, frilly skirts.

"But what's that, Aunt Sylvia?" she had asked once. "That horrible, long stick-thing?"

"That darling is a cane for when you're naughty. You and Mike."

"What does it do?"

"Silly child, haven't you ever seen a cane

before?" Shiny Sylvia laughed. "Uncle Archie smacks you on the bottom with it if you ever behave badly in this house ... or perhaps on your hands and then you stop. Behaving badly, I mean."

Nell was silent and bit her lip, knowing even then that Shiny Sylvia and she did not always agree about what was and what was not good behaviour. Seeing the cane there with all her favourite things spoilt the china cabinet for her and she avoided ever looking at it again.

"Why don't you both go and put your things away upstairs now?" Shiny Sylvia said, "and by the time you've done that, I daresay lunch will be ready."

Nell and Mike escaped gratefully and ran upstairs two at a time.

"Phew!" said Mike when the guest room door was closed behind them.

"I thought we'd never get up here ... what do you think she meant ... about Uncle Archibald coming home for lunch and telling us something?"

"Goodness knows ..." Nell was not listening properly. She was busy putting things from their suitcase into a drawer. "Hey Mike, I didn't know you'd packed the green glass bottle ... why did you?"

"I like it, that's why. I thought we might need it. I thought it might cheer us up. Give it to me."

He took it, and kneeling up on his bed, he put the bottle on the window sill. There was no sunlight, no lamplight to shine through the glass now, but even on this grey morning, it glowed with darkened secret colours.

"Yes," said Nell "it does make the room look better. But why should we need it?"

"I don't know. I think," Mike hesitated, "... because it's lucky."

Nell laughed. "You say the funniest things sometimes, but still I'm glad you brought it."

Mike looked out of the window.

"Will he do it, do you think? Mr Coronado? Will he come? How will he get in, d'you think?"

"By magic, of course," Nell said. "Come on Mike, we'd better go down now."

"Let's have a peep at the study on the way down."

"No, don't be stupid, we'll be caught and then we'd be in real trouble. Uncle Archibald's coming back for lunch, remember?"

"He might have left it unlocked by mistake."

"Never," said Nell. "It's never unlocked when he's out of the house."

"Well let's peep in through the keyhole on the way downstairs."

"OK, but hurry."

The children closed the door of their room as quietly as they could. Then they stepped softly across the landing. Not only was the door of Uncle Archibald's study locked, as it always was, but the keyhole had been blocked in some way since the children's last visit.

"Can't see a thing," muttered Mike.

"I don't think," said Nell, "there's anything to see."

"Then why keep it locked all the time?"

"Maybe he's got something valuable in there ..."

"Yeah. Stamps." Mike smiled. "That's why I'd love to get in ... just to have a look at what he's got hidden away. I'm sure he's never shown me everything he's got."

"Children!" Shiny Sylvia's voice glittered up the stairs. "Uncle Archie is here! Come and have lunch!"

Lunch was nearly over. The children had hardly
spoken at all. Uncle Archibald had grinned and
winked and chuckled and rubbed his suety hands
together throughout the meal like a man with a
pleasant secret. Now he was buttering water
biscuits and popping them into his mouth
covered with white cheese. He wiped the last
crumbs from his mouth and looked at Nell.

"Now, Eleanor my dear," he said, "and Michael. I
have to talk to you seriously. There are going to be
a lot of changes around here – changes for the
better, of course – and I think it's time you knew
all about them. Now of course you know this, but
I'll say it again because it's important. I'm a lawyer
by profession and this is lucky for you because if
there's anything you don't understand (any legal
terms, I mean) in what I am about to say, then you
can ask me what they mean and I'll explain them
to you. Ready? Right! Now the situation is that
when your parents died so tragically some years
ago we all searched high and low, but we couldn't
find a copy of their will. They'd made a will, all

such time as they reach the age of eighteen.
Archibald and Sylvia Gribbet are also to act as
trustees for the money which belongs to our
children, investing it as they think best.
Signed.
Henry Fenton and Victoria Fenton.'

This letter is dated one month before they took their last, fatal journey and would therefore invalidate any previously made will, even if we could find one, which of course we can't. Now that's all perfectly clear isn't it?"

"No," Nell and Mike said together.

"It means," said Uncle Archibald, "that you will live here with Sylvia and myself until you are eighteen ... of course, we'll send you both off to boarding schools, but basically ..."

Nell stood up. "No!" she shouted. "We can't ... It's not true ... It's impossible. They wouldn't. They could never have wanted that. They knew how much ..." Nell's voice faded away.

"How much what?" said Uncle Archibald, silkily.

Nell swallowed. "How much we loved Aunt Hatty." She sat down. She had been about to say, "how much we hated you", but stopped herself in time.

"The law, my dear," said Uncle Archibald, "is not concerned with could have and wouldn't have, but with reality, with black on white. And here it is, black on white. Sylvia and I are to have custody of you. I shall walk down to Hatty's with you when you go back to tell her the news. And now, my dears, I have a little work to do in the study ... perhaps later on you'd like to see some of my latest acquisitions in the stamp department."

"Thank you," said Mike automatically, but he wasn't really listening. Uncle Archibald left the room and Shiny Sylvia rustled along behind him.

Nell kicked Uncle Archibald's empty chair as hard as she could.

"Horrible, horrible, horrible little man. Stupid piece of paper. I'm sure it can't be true. I bet he and Shiny wrote it themselves, just to get their hands on us. Uncle Archibald would know how to make it look proper and legal and everything. They'll take us away from Aunt Hatty and lock us up in boarding schools with rice-pudding and cabbage every day. I can't believe it!"

"No one knows what they wanted for us. There wasn't any bit of paper then."

"If we come and live here, I bet they won't let us see Aunt Hatty again."

"I wish," said Mike, "I wish Uncle Archibald would lose that bit of paper. I don't see why he shouldn't."

"What do you mean?" Nell frowned.

"I expect he'll file that letter away upstairs ... if only we could get into the study, we could find the letter and burn it and then ..."

"Then nobody can say our parents wanted us to stay here ... Oh, Mike that's great ... but how can we do it? The study's always kept locked ... and Uncle Archibald has the keys ..."

"He doesn't generally lock it when he's in the house ... he's in and out of there the whole time ... we could go in while the news is on TV. They always watch that."

"OK. Ten o'clock then. But what if we're caught? They'll kill us."

"Do you want to live here till you're eighteen?"

"Don't be stupid," Nell said. "You know I don't."

"Then we haven't much choice, have we?" said Mike. "We'll have to search the study."

The white overhead light in the study snapped on, dazzling Nell and Mike as they stood beside the filing cabinet.

"So this," Uncle Archibald's voice was like ice, "is what you both get up to while we're watching the news ... snooping and ferreting about in other

people's belongings like common thieves ... yes, just like common criminals. What, may I ask, were you hoping to find?"

Nell said, "We were just going to have a look at the stamps, that's all."

"The filing cabinet is open. Were you hoping to find stamps under 'P' for "Philately' perhaps?" Uncle Archibald smirked. "No my dears, you'll have to do a little better than that. I shall give you the night to think it over. Either you come clean with me, or it's twelve strokes of the cane each – six on each hand – for sheer dishonesty allied to brazen cheek. Now get to bed, both of you. Not another word from either of you, please. It's clearly about time you learned the meaning of the word 'discipline'."

He turned and left the room, switching off the light and leaving Nell and Mike shivering in the dark.

At breakfast the next morning, Shiny Sylvia said,
"You're both very quiet today. I can't think why
you shouldn't be rejoicing. At last you'll be living as
heirs of Henry and Vicki Fenton. The way you
should be living, instead of scrimping in a seaside
boarding house ... Oh, and by the way, I'll be the
one to cane you. Archie will be busy with Mr
Coronado this morning."

Mike's knife clattered to the floor.

"Who?" he gasped.

"Do you *never* listen? A man called Coronado
... he's a foreign gentleman come to see Archie
about rare stamps or something. Whatever are you
laughing at? Have I said something funny?"

"No, Aunt Sylvia, I'm sorry," said Nell.

"Then stop being so silly and eat your toast."

The children ate, smiling happily at Shiny Sylvia
across the table.

"You will both," she said smiling back at them,
"come to the living room at half past eleven for
your punishment."

"Yes, Aunt Sylvia." Nell and Mike watched her as she left the room.

"He's here," Nell said, laughing. "Mr Coronado is here. Now everything will be better."

Mike said nothing, but he had had a feeling Mr Coronado was going to appear. He had dreamed all night of the clipper ship, white sails curved and swelling in a strong breeze, and a long white wake in a royal blue sea streaming behind her.

Shiny Sylvia unlocked the china cabinet and took out the cane. She swished it about in the air several times, enjoying the whooshing noise it made.

"I feel sick," whispered Mike.

Nell nodded, "Me too."

"Nell," Sylvia came towards them. "Nell, you stand here. And you over here, Mike. Now, who's going first?"

Nell looked at the snowy carpet. "I shall think myself out of this room", she said to herself, "and imagine that I am far away on an ice-covered plain."

"You first, Nell," said Sylvia, "as you're older."

Nell stepped forward, held her hands out and closed her eyes.

"Right," said Sylvia, "one, two, three ... oh, my goodness, how you startled me!"

"I'm very sorry, dear lady. I think I have mistaken the door. I was looking for Mr Gribbet's study." Nell opened her eyes and there was Mr Coronado standing in the doorway. "I see you are busy with these children," he said looking at Nell and Mike.

"Oh, that's fine, don't worry. This can wait. Nell, Mike, this is the gentleman I was telling you about, remember?"

"Yes, Aunt Sylvia," said Nell.

"What a beautiful collection of china, ma'am!" said Mr Coronado, looking closely at the cabinet.

"I'm a great admirer of such things myself."

"How delightful!" trilled Shiny Sylvia as she put the cane down on a chair. "Let me show you all my treasures."

"Nell," whispered Mike. "Just look at the cane!" The long, yellowish stick was sliding, slowly and silently off the chair.

"It's falling off," said Nell. "Should we put it back, d'you think?"

"Ssh! It's not falling off. It's going somewhere. Look!"

The cane slithered across the carpet to the very centre of the room. Then it stood upright. Nell and Mike looked at Mr Coronado. He was still facing the china cabinet, and his hands were clasped behind his back. The two thumbs were wriggling gently.

"Gosh, Mike, just look! The cane is growing into the carpet."

Nell stared as long roots began to burrow into the white pile, the thin stick grew fatter and small branches and leaves blossomed out of the top. After no more than a minute, a little tree with glossy green leaves stood in the middle of the room.

"And now Mr Coronado," said Sylvia as she
closed the cabinet, "I must get back to my sad task
of punishing these young people ... oh, goodness,
whatever is that?"

She peered at the tree. "There has never been a tree ..." She paused, turned pale and drew a deep breath. "Mr Coronado, I believe that a tree is growing in my carpet." She sat down very suddenly on the nearest chair.

"It is a lemon tree, I think," said Mr Coronado. "Carpets do sometimes do that, believe me."

"Really?" Shiny Sylvia's mouth was hanging open.

"Oh, yes, dear lady. No need to alarm yourself. I have seen carpets growing all manner of exotic things, jasmine, date palms, even cypress trees."

"Really?"

"Assuredly," said Mr Coronado. "Your lemon tree is, as they say, a mere bagatelle." He laughed. "It will transplant quite easily. I promise you, and be perfectly happy in your splendid garden."

"Perhaps I should do that before Archie sees it. He's ever so fond of this carpet and I don't think ..."

"Certainly, dear lady. I will find your husband and keep him occupied for a while. That will give you time to set the carpet to rights. It has been a pleasure. Good day to you. Goodbye, children."

"Goodbye," said Nell. "And thank you."

"Thank you," said Mike.

Mr Coronado closed the door behind him.

Shiny Sylvia stood up. "I shall get rid of that," she pointed at the tree, "and then I shall come back and cane you both. I'm going to get a spade and dig it up." Shiny Sylvia looked quite shaken under her glossy make up.

"Yes, Aunt Sylvia," said Nell. "We'll just wait here till you get back."

When she had gone, Mike smiled. "But she won't be able to find the cane, will she?"

"No, never," said Nell. "She'll never see it and it will be in the garden under her nose all the time. Lovely, lovely Mr Coronado!"

Nell and Mike joined hands and danced round the lemon tree until they were dizzy and out of breath.

"Listen," said Nell. "We must find Mr Coronado before he leaves the house and tell him everything ... he's the only one who can possibly help us ... we'll tell him what Uncle Archibald is planning and I'm sure, oh, I'm quite sure he'll know what to do ..."

"But what can he do?" Mike said. "He does a lot of magic, I know, but this ... this is ... different."

The door opened quite suddenly and Mr Coronado appeared. He was carrying his

Gladstone bag and wearing his hat.

"I have come to say my farewells, children," he began, but Nell and Mike ran towards him and seized him by the arms.

"You can't," Nell whispered. "You must stay and help us ... please. Something awful is going to happen to us if you don't."

"I suppose," he said, "you had better tell me all about it. Start at the beginning."

Archibald Gribbet's face was purple with rage.

"I had no idea that you were acquainted with these children. I should never have allowed you into the house, I can see that now. The whole idea is preposterous. Ludicrous! Unthinkable! Ridiculous!"

He paused and continued more quietly. "You are saying that I have deliberately hidden the Fenton will and forged the letter" (he patted the letter where it lay on his desk) "in order to get my hands on the money which will belong to these children. Nonsense! Impossible! I am a member of a respected and honoured profession."

"It is strange coincidence, though, is it not," said Mr Coronado, "that of all the wills, deeds, papers and documents filed away in this study, only the Fenton will should have been mislaid. Perhaps I could help you to find it."

"How do you reckon to do that, then?" Archibald Gribbet was now doing his best to smile.

"Like this," said Mr Coronado, and stretching both his hands in front of him, he lifted them high into the air, and then brought them down again.

At once, the drawers of the filing cabinet flew open and every piece of paper, every document out of every file from a cabinet full of papers, documents and files, moved as if swept by an enormous gust of wind, although no wind was blowing. A snowstorm of paper filled the room and drifted into piles on the floor. When all the paper had settled, one sheet still floated on the air, and fell at last, onto Archibald Gribbet's desk.

"Well, would you believe it," he said, pretending astonishment. "Here is the Fenton will at last, after all these years. Let me tell you what it says." He began to read to himself, muttering and snorting from time to time under his breath. Nell and Mike stared at him waiting, waiting to hear.

"Well, now," he said at last, "my dear little cousins and you sir, whatever sort of play-acting scoundrel you may be, first a philatelist and now some kind of wizard, you were all quite correct. This will does indeed give custody of the children to Miss Harriet Fenton."

"Then," Nell shouted, "it's all right. We can stay with Aunt Hatty. We won't have to leave. Oh, how lovely! Mike isn't it great?"

"I'm afraid," said Uncle Archibald, "that matters are not so easily settled."

"What do you mean, sir?" said Mr Coronado. "I have located the Fenton will, and its intention is absolutely clear."

"There is no Fenton will. You may swear to having seen it in the highest court in the land, but who will believe two children and a magician? Whereas *my* word, as a respectable lawyer, will, of course be respected, and, I say again, there is no Fenton will."

"But how can you?" burst out Mike. "It's there. It's in your hand."

Uncle Archibald's eyes sparkled, he laughed a gurgling, happy laugh and his suety hands moved quickly as he tore the will into a thousand tiny pieces. Nell and Mike stood, horrified, as he tossed the fragments over his head.

"You're not the only one," he chortled at Mr Coronado, well pleased at the joke, "who can create paper snowstorms!"

Nell strode to the open window and nearly crying with fury, she turned and looked at Archibald Gribbet.

"You are dreadful," she shouted. "You are the most dreadful person in the world. I wish a real storm would come and whisk you and every grotty bit of paper in this study right away for

ever. I wish it, I wish it, I wish it ... there." She stopped, out of breath. Mr Coronado twiddled his fingers a little, and looked at Mike, who was standing with his eyes tightly closed.

"Are you wishing, Mike?" Mr Coronado asked.

"Yes," said Mike, "as hard as I can."

"Heh! heh! heh!" Uncle Archibald was wiping tears of laughter from his eyes with a silk spotted handkerchief. "Nothing will help you now. Nothing."

As he spoke, a wind blew into the room and scattered some of the papers lying on the floor, then it whirled them upwards into a spiral and seemed to suck them out of the window.

"Papers! My files!" Uncle Archibald ran to catch them, but they flew out of his grasp and as he reached out, the wind seized him too, and pulled and sucked him over the sill, and gathered every scrap of paper in the study into a turning whirlpool of white that followed Uncle Archibald out of the window as a tail follows a kite.

The children ran to look. The garden was white with papers lying like small birds on the grass, and fluttering like wings in the sky. Far above the house, growing smaller and smaller as he flew higher and higher was the body of Uncle Archibald,

legs dangling, arms still clutching at the contents of his files. After a few moments, nothing could be seen of him. A cloud had swallowed him up and he was gone.

"Oh, Mr Coronado," said Nell, still leaning out of the window. "Thank you. You've done it. And we helped you, I'm sure. Do you think our wishing helped? We wished so hard, didn't we, Mike?"

Mike nodded without speaking, searching the sky for signs of a falling body, but seeing none.

Nell turned to look into the room. Mr Coronado was nowhere to be found.

"Mike, Mike, look, Mr Coronado's gone. Where is he? He's not here. He's left us and gone. Why, Mike, why? Why has he gone?"

"He's done what we asked," said Mike.

"Why didn't he wait and say goodbye to us? We never even thanked him."

"No," said Mike, "but we will."

"You're mad," said Nell. "Come on home now. We've got to get back to Hatty's as quickly as we can."

She walked out of the empty study and Mike followed her down the stairs.

Shiny Sylvia was standing in the hall.

"Have you two seen Archie?" she said. "I've looked for him everywhere ... and do you know anything about that paper all over the lawn? Where are you off to? Hey! Are you both quite mad? You've left your case ... come back ... Answer me, how dare you not answer me?"

The tide was high. Waves lapped against the wall, under the Promenade, as the children neared the Seaview Guest House. Mike stood up on the railings and threw the green glass bottle as far as he could into the sea.

"Where did that come from?" Nell asked.

"I put it in my pocket before breakfast," said Mike. "I knew we'd need it. There's that clipper ship again, look!"

"What clipper ship? Where? And why have you thrown away our lovely bottle?"

"I was thanking Mr Coronado. And the ship has gone now." Mike jumped down from the railing. "Let's go home."

Two months later a letter arrived at the Seaview Guest House addressed to Nell and Mike. Nell opened it and read the short note aloud:

"Dear Nell and Mike,

Mike, I know is a collector of stamps. The one on the envelope is rare. One could almost call it unique. I trust you are both happy.

Coronado.

That's nice isn't it, Mike? I've often wondered what happened to him and why we never heard."

"I'd like to see the stamp, Nell please."

"Stamp? Oh, yes, here it is." She handed the envelope to Mike who looked carefully at it, holding it up to the winter sunlight pouring through the kitchen window.

"Nell, come here quickly."

"What is it?"

"Look. Look at this stamp. It's him. It's really him. On the stamp."

"Who? Mr Coronado? Is he on it?"

"No, look."

Nell picked up the envelope. "Oh, yikes! it is him, isn't it?"

She giggled. "His mouth is still gaping pink like a goldfish and a worm. It's Uncle Archibald. Archibald Gribbet Transmogrified!"

"Trans-what?" Mike was laughing.

"Transformed. Changed. But it is him. Are you going to stick him in your album? This stamp hasn't got the name of a country on it."

"Then he'll have to have a page all to himself," said Mike, "but of course I'm going to stick him in. Nothing much else you can do with a stamp, really, is there?"

right, but even though I turned my chambers upside down not a trace of it could I find. I must also tell you, children, that in all my years as a lawyer this is the one and only time such a loss has occurred among my papers. So Fenton money passed to you because you were Henry and Victoria's only children. Of course you were much too young to be responsible for such a sum so we decided that the money was to be kept for you until you were grown up. The matter of custody ..."

"What's custardy?" said Mike, thinking of treacle puddings and apple pies.

"One who has custody of a child is the one who looks after him or her. Aunt Hatty has custody of you because you both wept and shrieked that that was where you wanted to live, and of course you were very young and had to be ... humoured on this occasion. Now, however, a document has come to light which will change all that. It is signed quite clearly by both your mother and your father. Tongle, my clerk, came across it in one of your father's books, which as you know, are being stored in my chambers. Would you like me to read it to you?"

"Yes, please," said Nell quietly. Mike said nothing.

"Very well then," said Uncle Archibald, "the letter reads,

 'We, the undersigned, being of sound mind, do hereby state that in the event of our deaths we would wish our children, Eleanor and Michael, to remain in the sole charge and custody of Archibald and Sylvia Gribbet until